JOSIE DANCES

This story began over forty years ago while watching my young daughter dance. Elders counsel us that to have the right to wear an eagle plume, we must first have our spirit name. In the powwow world we also have a "welcome to the circle" ceremony for the first time a child dances into the arena.

Migwech to the Greatwalker family for permission to put Grandma Greatwalker in the story. Huge thank-you to my writers group, Ok, Write! for their invaluable suggestions. Special thank-you to Angela Erdrich, whose collaboration on the paintings helped bring the story to life. Migwech to the powwow world, whose dance and songs feed my spirit and for continuing to welcome new dancers into the circle. —DL

Thank you to photographers Skip Baumhower for his powwow images and Wayne Perala for his bird images. His grace Mr. Emmett HisManyLightnings Eastman kindly allowed his image to be part of the powwow scene. Thank you to my artist mother, Rita Erdrich, for her lifelong advice and remarkable eye. Thanks to Denise Lajimodiere for sharing her beadwork designs and imagery ideas, and M. Judy Azure for allowing her beadwork and pottery images in Kookum's house. Many tribal and family members freely and kindly offered advice and encouragement. I am humbled by all the powwow artists who create inimitable and perfect beaded outfits that match from head to toe. —AE

mnhspress.org

The Minnesota Historical Society Press is a member of the Association of University Presses.

Manufactured in the United States of America.

10 9 8 7 6 5 4 3 2 1

∞ The paper used in this publication meets the minimum requirements of the American National Standard for Information Sciences—Permanence for Printed Library Materials, ANSI Z39.48-1984.

International Standard Book Number

ISBN: 978-1-68134-207-8 (hardcover)

Library of Congress Control Number: 2020950781

JOSIE DANCES

DENISE LAJIMODIERE

Illustrations by
ANGELA ERDRICH

MINNESOTA HISTORICAL SOCIETY PRESS

Josie wanted to dance at her tribal powwow.
She would need a fancy shawl outfit for her powwow debut.
She asked her mom, "Will you sew my dress and shawl?"
Mom said, "Eya, nindaanis!"

She asked her aunty, "Will you bead my cape?"
Aunty said, "Eya, ikwezens!"
She asked her kookum, "Will you bead my moccasins and leggings?"
Kookum said, "Eya, noozhishenh!"

Josie offered asemaa to tribal elder Grandma Greatwalker.
"Will you dream my spirit name?"
Grandma Greatwalker said, "Eya, abinoojiinh!"

All winter long they beaded and sewed.
All winter long Josie practiced her dance steps.
All winter long Grandma Greatwalker prayed
   for a name.

Josie leaned on her mom's knee. "Are you
done with my dress and shawl?"
Mom shook her head. "Gawiin, nindaanis."
Josie skipped to her aunty's house. "Are you
done with my cape?"
Aunty shook her head. "Gawiin, ikwezens."

Josie asked her kookum, "Are you done with
my moccasins and leggings?"
Kookum shook her head. "Gawiin,
noozhishenh."
Josie asked Grandma Greatwalker, "Have
you dreamed my name?"
Grandma Greatwalker shook her head.
"Gawiin, abinoojiinh."

Spring birds returned, and
Juneberries ripened.
Soon it would be time for the
summer powwow.

Josie worried a little bit, but
she kept busy practicing
her fancy shawl steps in
the living room.

Then, finally, it was camp day.
Josie helped put up the tent and made beds
    while listening to drummers practicing,
    the announcer doing mic *check*, *check*, *check*,
    children laughing, and
    the happy cries of visitors seeing family.
The aroma of delicious fry bread wafted through camp.

Stretched out on her bed,
   Josie thought of the powwow circle.
Would her outfit be done in time?
Or would she have to wait another year?

The next morning, when Josie stepped out of the tent,
sleepy-eyed, her hair shakaweesh,
she saw an eagle flying above the trees.
"Me, me, take me!" Josie cried to Migizi.
Oh, how she wished she could fly like an eagle.

"Ambe Josie!" her mom called.

"Namadabi; come sit so I can braid your hair."

Then Josie remembered, and she hung her head.

Where was Grandma Greatwalker?

Where was her cape?

Where were her leggings and moccasins?

Where was her dress?

When her hair was braided, Josie looked up.
There was Grandma Greatwalker!
And Aunty holding her cape.
And Kookum with her leggings and moccasins.
Her mom smiled and held up her dress and shawl.
Grandma Greatwalker came forward.
"In my dream I saw a young eagle flying. You are
   Migiziinsikwe, Young Eagle Woman!"
As she spoke, Grandma tied a fluffy white plume
   in Josie's hair.
"The eagle carries our prayers to the Creator.
   Wear this plume with grace and honor."

Now, on this sunny August day,
   it was time for the ceremony.
Josie stood in the arena as family
   gathered behind her.
When the drum began her honor song, the
   audience rose up.
"Hey-hey-ah-hey!" the announcer called out.
"Let's give Josie a big powwow welcome!"

She heard the singers say
    her name, Migiziinsikwe.
As she danced
    into the circle
    people came
    and shook her hand.

Then the drum beat faster!

*"Dancers: join in! Welcome
    Josie to the powwow world!"*

Wearing brightly colored
   beadwork, ribbons, and shawls,
   sequined dancers swirled
as they entered the arena,
   their jingles, fringe, and feather bustles
flying as they circled round.

Grandma Greatwalker, dancing near,
   whispered in Josie's ear.

"Listen to the drum, the heartbeat of Aki.
   You are dancing for the ancestors
      and all the people that you see."

Josie whirled,
twisted,
swirled!

On the drum's last
    singing beat, her beaded
    moccasin feet
    stopped on time.
She held one arm high
    and dipped the other toward
    earth, her shawl fringe
    twirling into the shape
    of eagle wings.

Young Eagle Woman soared!

Glossary

Abinoojiinh Child
Aki Mother Earth
Ambe Come
Asemaa Tobacco made from red willow
Bustle Part of a man's dance regalia
Eya Yes
Gawiin No
Ikwezens Young girl
Kookum Grandmother
Migizi Bald Eagle
Migiziinsikwe Young Eagle Woman
Namadabi Sit

Nindaanis My daughter
Noozhishenh Granddaughter
Plume Fluffy eagle feather, worn by both men and women.
Powwow A gathering or celebration where Native people from all tribes dance together
Shakaweesh Messy hair; sticking up all over
Shawl A length of material with fringe around the edges, worn by women, especially fancy shawl dancers

Turtle Mountain is a small reservation located in north-central North Dakota near the Canadian border. It is home to the Plains Ojibwe and Metis/Michif people. It's a beautiful place with many freshwater lakes and Sibising, locally known as "the little creek that sings," flowing through the middle of the reservation. The low-lying hills, similar to a turtle's carapace, are covered in aspen, birch, elm, poplar, bur oak, and thick brush. Travelers coming from the south can see the turtle's head facing to the west. The turtle's body is where the towns of Dunseith and Belcourt lie, and the turtle's tail lies to the east, near the town of Rolla.

Turtle Mountain

Canada

North Dakota

Bear Butte

Butte St Paul

map of Turtle Mountain after cartography of Capt. W.J. Twining 1869